# The Nightmare Card

## by

## Catherine Johnson

To my family

First published in 2011 in Great Britain by
Barrington Stoke Ltd
18 Walker Street, Edinburgh, EH3 7LP

www.barringtonstoke.co.uk

ISBN: 978-1-84299-828-1

Printed in China by Leo

# Contents

# Chapter 1
# In the Cards

Sara Edwards used to be my best friend. We were the sort of friends who did everything together. We even imagined we'd still be best friends when we were grown ups. We would go on holiday together and be bridesmaids at each other's weddings. Mina and Sara, best friends for ever.

My mum said we were like sisters. Five years of being best friends, from Year Three in Green End Primary to last summer, when we were in Year Eight at Elm Court High School. The last day of that Spring Term was the last time anyone saw Sara.

The police told her mum she could have run off, found a boy she liked or maybe gone to her dad's on the coast. But she still has no idea where Sara is. No one has. Except me, and I still don't want to believe it.

I shiver sometimes when I walk past her house. I suppose I should count myself lucky because we're moving soon and maybe then I'll be able to forget. Sara's mum is still here. She stands at the window looking out, as if Sara is going to come walking down the street any minute. If she sees me she comes out. Her eyes are always red and puffy, as if she hasn't stopped crying since Sara vanished.

"Have you heard anything, Mina? Has she called you? Sent you a text?" she asks. And I can't bear to look at her because she looks so sad. So I just shake my head and walk away as quick as I can.

Sometimes I think I see Sara in the crowd at school when the bell goes. A pixie-faced girl with short blonde hair and light brown eyes, pushing past the people in the corridor. Or up at the shops on a Saturday. But when I get close it's never her.

The police have asked me over and over. They've even taken our computer to check I wasn't hiding any secret emails or anything. I told them we'd stopped talking in May, that she wouldn't tell me anything ever again, but they took no notice. I've told them what I know at least ten times. Over and over. And when I go to bed sometimes it's all I think about – Sara.

The police don't believe me. I know that for a fact. Every time I've told them what happened I can see the looks they give each other, like they think I'm nuts, or hiding something, or both. *Girls don't vanish because of a pack of cards*, that's what they're thinking. And it's true, I'd have thought just the same not so long ago.

And you don't have to believe me either.

But I've written it all down. Everything. Just the way it was. So you can make up your own mind. See what you think happened. Just because it sounds like something out of one of those late night spooky films doesn't mean it isn't all true.

# Chapter 2
# The Nightmare Card

I was out of breath when I reached Sara's. "I beat your record! Two minutes forty five seconds," I said, checking my watch as the door opened. Only it wasn't Sara. I felt myself blushing.

"We do this thing, Karen," I panted, trying to explain to Sara's mum. "Racing each other from door to door."

"I do know all about you two," she said. She gave me a hug. "Happy New Year, Mina!

Go up, but only for five minutes. We've only just got back from Gran's and you have school tomorrow. I don't want anyone getting into trouble for arriving late."

I ran upstairs and went into Sara's bedroom. "Two minutes forty five ..." I said. I stopped, feeling a bit babyish and stupid. Sara was sitting on the floor, not on her bed on the pink satin quilt, or at her desk on the computer.

"What are you doing?" I said. She had a pack of cards in her hand, but they were odd-looking. They were bigger than playing cards and the pictures on them weren't the usual ones – hearts and clubs and that. Sara was taking slow deep breaths and her eyes were shut tight.

"I'm seeking something out," Sara said.

"Seeking out what?" I said.

"My powers. So I can read your fortune."

"What?" I said, sitting down on the floor facing her.

"With the cards. These are special. They're called Tarot Cards. I got them from my Aunty Rachel. She's gone to live in Australia." She opened her eyes. "They can tell the future. It really works!"

"Come off it, Sara." I made a face. "You always laugh at Charley when she reads the star signs in her mag."

We both used to laugh when we heard Charley reading out what was going to happen to her and her mates. But we didn't do it in front of Charley. She was the sort of girl to thump you in the cloakroom if she thought you were making fun of her. She and her gang were not to be messed with.

"Yeah, well, Charley doesn't know anything." Sara made a face. "This is different. Look. I'll show you. This is *real*."

"OK." I crossed my arms. "Go on, then."

"No, you have to ask the cards a question," Sara said, shuffling them as she talked.

"What? Like, 'what's on at the cinema next week?'" I said.

"Don't be daft. No, you know, 'will this be a good year?' That kind of thing."

I rolled my eyes. I didn't want to do this. I knew it wasn't quite the same as when we went on the school trip in Year Seven and some of the girls wanted to call up ghosts in the bathroom mirrors. But it still felt ... wrong? *Not right at all.* It made me feel uneasy.

I sighed. I wanted to talk about the sort of parts we might get in the school play and if she thought it would be worth walking to school the long way round so we would bump into Levi.

"I know!" Sara said and looked right at me. "Ask them about Levi! Go on! Ask them."

"You must have been reading my mind ..." I grinned, but I knew I sounded a bit nervous.

"OK, OK, then. Does Levi like me?" I said, feeling myself go pink when I said his name out loud.

Sara took a deep breath and shuffled the pack again. She held it out to me and I turned over the first card.

"I don't believe this stuff, you know," I said. I looked at Sara as I took a card and turned it over. She was smiling – a small, calm smile.

I looked at the card. It showed a young man wearing old-style clothes. Like something off the posters for *Romeo and Juliet* in the English room.

"Page of Cups," she said.

"What does that mean then, clever clogs?"

"Well it's just got to be Levi. Turn another one. Go on."

I did. Sara gasped. "The Lovers."

For a tiny second my heart jumped. The picture showed a man and a woman with flowers all round them. "The Lovers! Oh, my days!" Sara said, sounding amazed. She looked at me and her eyes were two circles. "You better believe it, Mina! You and Levi! It's in the cards."

For a minute I said nothing, because, in spite of everything I had just said, I did so want to believe it. I wanted to believe that me and Levi were going to get together. I wanted to believe it really badly. I felt my mouth drop open. I looked at both the cards. The young man, and the lovers.

There was a noise – well – it sounded like a fart, but when I looked up at Sara, she was trying not to laugh. When she saw me looking she just let it out, a rolling bubbling laugh.

"Your face!" she said in between giggles. "You should have seen it!"

At first I was angry. Angry I had fallen into her trap so easily. Angry that I had let myself believe in all that rubbish.

"I never thought anything," I said, crossing my arms.

"You did! You did! I'm so sorry, Mina, but you were a picture. And that was so easy! I knew you'd ask about Levi!"

"I'm going," I said, getting up.

"Come on, Mina! I never meant it. I know you like Levi and I couldn't resist it." She tugged me back down. "Oh, come on, Mina, think about it! If it works on you, I could do Levi and tell him he was going to meet a small, dark, beautiful girl and he should ask her out."

"No! Don't you dare!" I said. "Don't you dare!"

"Mina! Course I wouldn't. But we can have loads of fun telling fake fortunes with these. You know some of the girls in school, they'll believe anything!"

"So you don't really believe it, then?"

"Course not! I just put the cards in the order I knew you'd pick them up. Simple as that."

"But I saw you shuffling them!"

"Yeah, well you weren't watching me close enough were you? People *want* to be tricked. That's what Aunty Rachel said and it looks like she was right!"

Sara spread the cards out face up. In all of them the people wore strange, old-style clothes. Some were happy – families dancing under a rainbow, while others were really nasty – a tower struck by lightning, and the Death Card, a grinning skeleton dressed in armour. Sara must have seen my face.

"Oh, Death's not so bad," she said. "It's not even the worst card. People don't understand that. Death can mean the end of something but also a new start, a change. This is the one that really gives me the creeps. Nine of Swords. Nasty." She pulled out a card and laid it in front of me. "They call it the Nightmare Card."

She was right – it was horrible. A woman was sitting upright in bed, her hands over her face as if she was crying, or as if she was terrified. In the dark of her room nine swords hung in the air. They weren't pointing at her or anything. Even though you couldn't see her face at all, just her dark brown hair down over her shoulders, there was something really sad about the picture. Sad and terrifying.

I turned it over quick, so I didn't have to look at it.

"Look, Sara," I said. "Are you sure this is a good idea? Just because *I'm* stupid enough to trust you ..."

It wasn't just that I was worried about whether the card told the truth or not. That picture had really given me the creeps. It didn't feel right. I didn't want Sara to think that I believed in the cards even more now. I knew Sara would laugh at me.

Just then, her mum shouted up that it was time for me to go. I said I'd knock for Sara in the morning and we could decide then who would get the 'treatment' first.

It took ages to get to sleep. For a tiny second I thought of the horrible picture of the girl on the card, sitting bolt upright in bed, crying. I turned over and shut my eyes tight. I told myself I was just excited and nervous to be going back to school. The holidays had been long and boring, just me and Mum and Dad, Mum worrying that Dad might lose his job. She could moan for England, my mum.

I crossed my fingers hoping we would bump into Levi and imagining that he would ask me out. Sara wouldn't dare do the cards on him and drop me in it, would she? I crossed the fingers on my other hand.

I hoped she wouldn't wind Charley up too much. If Charley found out Sara was treating her like a fool, her life, and my life, wouldn't be worth living.

Now, when I look back, I wish I'd tried a bit harder to get Sara interested in something else.

# Chapter 3
# The Future's Bright

Every lunch break was pretty much the same at Elm Court High School. We'd queue up far too long for the usual range of rubbery pizzas, sandwiches with too many slimy slices of tomato, or chips that seemed to have been made out of plastic potatoes. Then there was the half hour spent seeing if we could find Levi and his mate Danny and stalking them, hoping they didn't notice.

It was worse if it was really wet or cold. Then we'd sit in the library where Queen Bee Charley and her mates would suck up to Mrs Drew, the librarian. And when Mrs Drew was looking the other way or eating biscuits in her office, they'd torment the Year Sevens. I saw them once take some poor boy's Art folder off him and throw his work around. They laughed at his superhero drawings, said they were baby rubbish, and they made him cry, in front of everyone!

Sara and I would try and keep out of the way, shivering by the glass windows or squashed in the corner with the art books. But once Sara started bringing the cards to school, everything changed for us, for the better.

Sara was playing with the cards in the library, shuffling them – that's what it looked like, anyway, if you didn't know what she was doing. Charley was sitting at the next table along with her friend Dee, pretending she wasn't watching.

"Want me to do you?" Sara said, and Charley shrugged like she wasn't interested but you could tell she was. Sara held the pack out. "Go on, pick one."

Charley looked down her nose at the pack, like she thought it might be infected, but she took a card anyway. It was a woman kneeling under a star with a jug in each hand. Sara's eyes went huge and she gasped. "The Star," she said, making it sound like she was really amazed.

Charley looked puzzled. "Is that bad or something?"

"No ... no. You hardly ever get that one come up ... it's brilliant, it's like you're really talented," said Sara. I nodded, trying not to smile.

"Yeah, well she is," said Dee. Dee didn't look impressed at all, but Charley wasn't even pretending not to be interested any more. I couldn't help thinking how easy it was to fool someone if you told them just what they wanted to hear.

"No," Sara said. "It means you'll do really well. It's like, your future's shining ..."

"Like a star?" Charley said.

"Could be," I said, trying to sound deep and serious the way Sara did. "Take another one, go on."

Charley didn't stop to think this time.

"The Two of Cups!" said Sara. "That's romance!"

"Romance?"

"Yeah, but it also stands for beauty and power." Sara was smiling, like she really really wanted to see what the cards would say about Charley's future. "Try another one – ooh, the Seven of Pentacles! That means success, you're gonna be rich!" Sara put that card down next to the others, a man leaning on a stick looking over what looked like a plant growing big yellow coins with stars on them.

"Take one more," Sara told Charley. "Go on, I mean I've never seen them like this before ... they're all so good!"

Charley took another and laid it out.

"Oh, my days!" Sara squeaked. "The Sun!"

"What's that mean? I'm gonna be in the paper?" Charley said. She was joking, but you could tell she really wanted to know what it meant.

"Maybe," said Sara. "It's a really good card, Charley, it means a bright future, self-confidence ... maybe you should go on *The X Factor!*"

Dee leaned forward, her eyes wide. "Do me next!"

After that, Sara and I had a place at the big table in the library, whether it was raining or not. Mrs Drew would look at us over the top of her glasses like she had an idea what was going on, but she never said a thing.

I was worried at first that Sara would leave me out, that the whole thing had been a way to get into Charley's group, to move into the popular crowd and leave me behind. But Sara needed me. Anyone in Year Eight could tell what Charley wanted out of life. But her mates were all a little different. That was my job. Sara knew how good I was at watching and listening, well we both were, but now she had moved into the in-crowd, it was up to me to get the information on everyone else. Just little things – who they fancied or whether they wanted money or fame or both. I found out if they were going on holiday to Florida in the summer, or would be lucky to get a day trip to Wherever-on-Sea, so that Sara knew which cards to pull.

And to tell the truth I quite enjoyed it. Before, if we walked up from the canteen to the Year Eight form rooms, no one spoke to Sara or me.  They didn't even look at us.  It was as if we just didn't exist.  Sometimes I thought I could have walked around that school with no clothes on and no one would have noticed.  But now we were both somebody.  We were the girls with the cards.  Well, OK, Sara was the girl with the cards, I was the girl with the cards' mate.  But that was cool.  Better than cool.

After a few weeks with the cards even Levi noticed me.

It was a filthy wet day in April.  The rain lashed down the glass windows of the library and there were so many people crammed inside to keep warm that Mrs Drew had given up trying to keep any kind of order.  Sara was over on the big table reading the cards for Charley's boyfriend, Dean from Year Nine, when Levi smiled at me.  I felt so hot that I thought the sun had come out but then I remembered I was sitting next to the radiator.

"You don't believe all that stuff, do you?" he said. "I thought you and Sara had more sense."

I froze. What could I say?

"Well ..." I said, after what seemed like an hour of silence.

Levi put on a spooky voice. "I can see a tall dark stranger ..."

I laughed. Which is hard to do when you're blushing.

"Are you doing anything on Saturday?" he said.

# Chapter 4
# Fool Me Twice

"I told you the cards were true, didn't I?" Sara said to me when we were walking home.

"You told me you made it all up! You told me you put the cards in the order you wanted! Sara! You haven't got second sight!" I said. "If you remember, it *is* me who gets you all the information and you who sits there with the cards telling them what they want to hear."

"Mina, calm down." Sara was sounding less and less like her old self. There was something in the way she looked at me, too, it was the way she looked at people when she did their fortunes, that sort of smug, smiling face that said she knew everything and they didn't.

She looked down the street to check no one else was around. She took a deep breath.

"Mina, I can't explain. It *was* all made up at first, really." She shrugged. "But now I don't even have to put them in any kind of order at all. They always come up right. And I just sort of know what to say. It all comes into my head. Just like that." She snapped her fingers.

I felt cold. "Sara, stop it. That is daft." I started walking away fast, but Sara chased after me.

"No! It's true. Didn't you see me with Dean? You only found out the name of his brother's band for me, but the cards showed me loads more. I knew his dad's name and I know that the school football team are going to come second in the county league." She took another deep breath. "I even know he's going to break up with Charley over the holidays and that he's going to pass his Maths GCSE the year after next, but I didn't say that out loud."

"Come off it, Sara!" I was getting angry again.

Sara held my arm.

"I'll show you."

"You're not going to fool me again!"

Back in her room she lit a joss stick and I made a face. It smelled thick and heavy.

"I've been practising, Mina." Sara said.

I didn't say anything.

"Look, I know. At first I was like you, but it's different now. I really can see the future."

I looked right into her face.

"Honest. The cards don't lie," she said, and she looked like the old Sara again, just for a second. "You *have* to believe it!"

"I don't have to believe anything!"

Sara sighed and started shuffling the cards. "So what are you going to ask them?"

I thought for a bit. I was longing to know about Levi but I thought that was asking for trouble. Anyway, I didn't want to rub it in about Levi and me, not when I knew his mate Danny hardly noticed Sara ... and it had to be something Sara didn't know about, so she wouldn't be able to guess it. Not about me, but about my family. I took a deep breath. "My mum," I said. "She's worried about Dad losing his job. So. Will he?"

Sara nodded. She laid out the cards, a different pattern this time, like the numbers on a clock.

"This," she turned over the King of Cups, "is the card that stands for your dad, and this ..." she said turning over another, "is what has gone before."

The card was the happy family under a rainbow. I gulped – so far so good.

"This," Sara turned over the next card, "is what is going on right now."

The picture showed a young woman and a lion. There were flowers and the sky was blue. The word across the bottom read 'Strength'.

"Your parents must be strong. Times are hard. You must be strong too, stronger than everyone," Sara said. I felt the anger bubbling up inside, this was just rubbish, the sort of general stuff that you could get from your star sign in a mag. This was Sara pulling my leg again.

"Sara?" I said. "Are you jealous of me and Levi? Because this," I pointed at the cards, "isn't telling me anything I don't know already."

Sara flashed a look at me and I froze. It was as if I was looking at someone else.

"Wait!" Even her voice sounded different. "This is what is to come."

She turned over another card. I gasped. It was the Tower Struck by Lightning. That was the worst card in the whole pack, worse than Death. Disaster, tragedy, all the bad stuff.

She looked at me and there was real sadness in her face.

"He loses his job. You lose your house. Your friendship with someone close. Your world turns upside down."

"What! Are you nuts?"

"It's worse for your mum, you know." She twisted up her face. "Your parents might even split up. I can't see that far ahead. It's sort of cloudy ..."

"Sara, stop it!" I didn't want to hear any more.

"And it's going to be even worse for my mum. I can't see what she loses ... but you only lose a friend."

"What? What's your mum got to do with anything? Oh, and I lose a friend, do I? Let me guess! You know your problem Sara? You're just jealous!" I said. "You and your stupid cards!" I knocked the rest of the cards out of her hand and they flew up into the air and all over the place. They went everywhere, on the floor, on the desk, one had fallen on my coat where I'd left it on Sara's bed. For a quick second I saw it was the Nightmare Card, the woman in bed with nine swords hanging in the air. The quilt on the bed in the card was pink and shiny, just like Sara's. Was it like that before? I looked at her but her face was still and cool. Like she didn't care about anything.

I ran out of her room and down the stairs. She didn't even say sorry.

When I got home, Mum and Dad were there already, sitting at the kitchen table, pale and sad-looking.

Mum didn't need to tell me what had happened. Dad's firm had gone bust and he'd lost his job. Sara had said it would be bad and she was right, the cards were right. Mum said she wasn't sure yet but we might have to move.

I ran upstairs and lay on my bed. I think I would have cried all night if Levi hadn't texted me.

# Chapter 5
# Change is Coming

I walked in with Levi the next morning. It was so good to have someone else to talk to. But I couldn't take my mind off Sara and the cards.

"She just got lucky," Levi said. "Loads of firms are going out of business, it's all over the news. I expect she just made a clever guess."

I knew he was right but I couldn't shake the feeling it wasn't that simple. I didn't say anything because I didn't want to look stupid when he was being so sensible about it. But it must have been clear I was still worried because he gave me a comforting smile and said, "She's just mucking about. You just need to make it up with her and you'll both feel better."

But Sara was off school for nearly a week, and I didn't get any email messages from her on my computer and she didn't text me. I was beginning to get worried when she turned up at the end of the week.

"Sara!" I was so pleased to see her sitting in our form room that I ran over and hugged her – I had forgotten about the row, I was just happy to see her. She didn't hug me back.

"You never texted me!" I said. I thought she'd say sorry too for not being in touch and we'd laugh but she didn't. I took a deep breath. Maybe she didn't hear. "Sara, look, I'm sorry, OK?" I spoke softly. I didn't want the whole class hearing. "I didn't mean to storm off and that."

She turned towards me and I could see she was pale, and there were dark circles under her eyes as if she hadn't slept for a week. She put her hand on my arm and I could see that her nails were bitten right down.

"Sara? Are you OK?" Maybe she was still a bit ill. That would make sense.

"The cards." She said after a while. "They were right weren't they? About your dad ..."

"Yes, Sara they were – "

"See!" Sara hissed at me.

Are you sure you're all right?" I said.

"I'm fine," she snapped. Maybe it wasn't going to be so easy to make up.

The bell went and Charley linked her arm through Sara's and swept her away towards the next lesson.

I didn't go to the library at break. The sun was shining and I needed to get some air. I knew something had changed about Sara and I knew it wasn't to do with her and Charley or me and Levi. I made up my mind to go round after school whether she asked me or not.

********

"Mina! It's so good to see you!" Sara's mum hugged me tight. "I was worried you and Sara had fallen out. She hasn't been herself, you know ..."

Her mum thought so too. It wasn't just me.

"Is Sara upstairs?"

"No," her mum said. "But you go up and wait, she won't be long."

It felt as if I hadn't been in Sara's room for a year let alone a week. Everything was the same, but it felt cold somehow. The pictures on the wall were the same, the same shiny pink quilt, her hair clips and her old cuddly bunny on her bedside table. The laptop was shut on her desk ... the Tarot cards in a neat pile.

I wished I could cut them up or throw them away or flush them down the loo. I wished her aunt had never given them to her. She hadn't been the same since Christmas, I swear it.

I picked the pack up. I half expected an electric shock or some weird voice to come out of nowhere and tell me to put them down. Nothing happened. They were just cards, old-style pictures on bits of card, nothing more. Sara was fooling herself and everyone else. Even the Tower Struck by Lightning didn't look scary in the day-light. It was all chance. Levi was right.

Downstairs, the door slammed and I could hear someone running upstairs. I put the cards back and picked the phone out of my pocket and pretended to text someone. When

Sara came in I saw her eyes flick over to the cards.

"Hi, Sara! Your mum said it was OK ..."

"Yeah. Hi." Sara picked the cards up and held them tight. She still looked pale, and the dark circles round her eyes looked as if someone had been hitting her.

"Sara, look, I'm sorry. You're my best friend ..."

Sara laughed.

"You *are* my best friend!" I said again.

"So why don't you call for me in the mornings any more?" she said. "Levi Hibbert more interesting?"

"Sara! It's got nothing to do with Levi, you know that! Anyway, you seem to prefer Charley to me these days!" I felt bad as soon as I'd said it.

We said nothing. Sara shuffled the cards in her hand over and over.

"You could stop messing with those things!" I said.

Sara laughed again. It was a bit of a mad laugh and I tried not to show that I was scared. How could I be scared? She was my best friend. I'd known her forever.

"What's so funny?" I said.

Sara shuffled the cards. "You don't get it, do you? The cards know the future, Mina, really they do. They are special."

I sighed. Sara went on. Her voice wasn't scary. It was scared.

"Mina, I was like you! I was, at first. I didn't believe them. But I can't stop it now. I can't stop them. Look."

She cut the cards, and turned the top card over. It was the Nine of Swords, the Nightmare Card.

"See?" she shuffled, cut the pack again, then showed me the card. "It's always the same."

The Nightmare Card. The picture of the girl sitting up in bed, nine swords hanging in the air. I looked close – the quilt was shiny pink, just like Sara's.

"Oh, my God!" I said. "It's your bed! It's your room! How did you do that? On the computer or something? Come on! Stop mucking around."

"I wish I was." Sara shuffled again and cut the pack a third time. She turned over the top card and I gasped. There it was again. The woman in bed, hands over her face, the swords hanging in the air.

"Mina, I can't stop it!" There were tears welling up in her eyes. "And look! In the

Nightmare Card. It *is* my bed isn't it? You can see that."

"It looks like your bed ..." I said, peering at the picture. "But it can't be, not really ..." I was kidding myself. There on the card was Sara's quilt and there was her bedside table. There were her hair clips and her old toy bunny.

I took it from her, and held the card close to see if she'd drawn on it or fixed the picture somehow. No. It *was* Sara's bedroom on the card. Sara's bedroom with nine metal swords hanging in the air above Sara's bed. A strange woman with long brown hair sitting upright as if she was crying or terrified or both.

"Something's happening, Mina ..." Sara said. "Something bad is happening ..." The look on her face was strange, she looked scared, but there was something odd about it too, something I didn't trust.

"Come off it, Sara, you're just trying to wind me up again! Silly old Mina falls for it every time."

"I'm not! It's the cards!"

"The cards are stupid! I said so right from the start! I told you not to mess with them! They've driven you nuts!" I went over to the door but suddenly Sara had got there first. She stood there with her hand on the door. She wouldn't let me pass.

"Sara! What are you doing? Get away."

"No. You have to stay." She hissed the words out and I was scared. "The cards *are not* stupid! They are the truth!"

"Let me go!" She didn't move. "I will shout," I said. We were face to face. I could see her eyelids twitching. "You've changed, Sara. You really have."

I'm ashamed to say I pushed her away and ran down the stairs and all the way home.

That was the last time I saw her. Sort of.

# Chapter 6
# After

I went into school with Levi the next day and the day after that until it was just what I did every day. One day we were walking home as usual, when Sara's mum came out of the house, her eyes red and full of tears.

"Mina! There you are! Have you seen Sara?"

As soon as she said the words I felt a chill, as if my bones had been dipped in ice. Levi must have felt it too, because he gripped my hand tighter.

"No, not for ages."

"Has she texted you, called you?"

"No.  Why, what's happened?" I said.

"She's missing, Mina.  Sara's missing!"

We went into the house and Levi made some tea while I got Sara's mum to call the police.  I sat with her, rubbing her back the way my mum rubbed mine when I was upset. She was shaking.  Levi came in with tea.

"I've put lots of sugar in it, Karen," he said. "Look, I don't mean to make you worry, but have you checked her passport's not gone?"

"No, I mean yes.  Her passport's here."

"I could check her computer for you if you like, Karen," I said.

"Could you? Oh, Mina! Maybe there's something there!"

I went upstairs. Her room was almost just the same as it had been the last time I'd been round. The bed was neat, the shiny quilt pulled straight. The hair clips and old bunny on the bedside table. Her computer closed on her desk. The pack of cards stacked beside it.

I heard Sara's mum come up the stairs.

"I don't think she can be far," I said. "All her stuff is here."

I knew her password but there was nothing on the computer – no secret boyfriends, nothing about running away. The doorbell rang and Sara's mum went downstairs to open it. I could hear it was the police.

I picked up the cards, held them in my hands and shuffled them.

Without thinking I turned the top one over. It was the Nightmare Card.

I heard myself gasp.

The woman in the bed had changed. It wasn't a woman at all, it was a girl, a girl my own age, a girl with short blonde hair. She sat bolt upright in bed, in a bed with a shiny pink quilt, hands covering her face like she was terrified. Nine swords hung in the air above her head.

I felt my knees give way under me and I had to put my hand out to stop myself from falling. I knew where Sara was. She hadn't gone far at all. That was Sara trapped in the Nightmare Card.

Barrington Stoke would like to thank all its readers for commenting on the manuscript before publication and in particular:

Stuart Barr
David Wilsun Cooper
Rebecca Devine
Martin Frame
Kariss Gallagher
Jacqueline MacCallum
Liam Smith McDonald
Josh McNeill
Daniel Rae
Liam Scott
Jamie-Louise Wilson

### The Fall
### by
### Anthony McGowan

Mog might be a loser, but he's not as much of a loser as Duffy. So when Duffy tries to get in with Mog's best mate, Mod decides to take action. But when he lands Duffy in The Beck, the rancid stream behind school, Mog has no idea how far the ripples will spread...

### Wolf
### by
### Tommy Donbavand

Adam didn't have much planned for this afternoon – head home from school, grab a snack, maybe play a video game. No way did he plan to grow some claws. Or fur. Or a tail. At this rate, Adam will be having his mum and dad for tea. And they don't seem exactly surprised...

You can order these books directly from our website at
www.barringtonstoke.co.uk

### Pirate Attack!
### by
### Paul Dowswell

It was supposed to be the holiday of a lifetime. Now it's a fight for life. When Dan's family win a sailing holiday he asks Joe to join them for two weeks of sun, sea and sand.
But then Somali pirates board their boat and it seems like they might just get a bullet to the head. Joe needs a plan – and fast...

### Bad Day
### by
### Graham Marks

Rob's going to meet Tessa. Like, for real. In person. For the first time. Then Rob starts to think twice. And what should have been a great day begins to fall apart, big style...

You can order these books directly from our website at
www.barringtonstoke.co.uk